Rambles On!

BOOK #2

Oh, and Another Thing...

by Karen Salmansohn

Tricycle Press
Berkeley/Toronto

A Crash Course in Crushes

You see that page over there? ⟶

That page is **1,000,001%** dedicated to **Max**. Meaning, this is a page meant for kissing— which I am now doing, pretending this page is Max himself! • And you can bet I am trying very hard not to give him **Aunt Harriet Kisses**. NOTE: my Aunt Harriet is always planting these **embarrassingly** LOUD "**Mwaaah**!" kisses on everyone. • UGH • My **biggest** fear: If ever I am lucky enough to be kissed by Max, I'm worried that my Aunt Harriet's super loud kissing dysfunction is a genetic spasm that runs in our family and I too will make this **Mwaaah** sound. • So, I had this idea: practice kissing on a piece of paper. • I open my eyes from kissing practice now— and sadly see I am merely kissing paper. • That's when I have another idea. • I will draw Max's face on another page so I can **REALLY** imagine I am kissing him.

HERE is Max NOW...

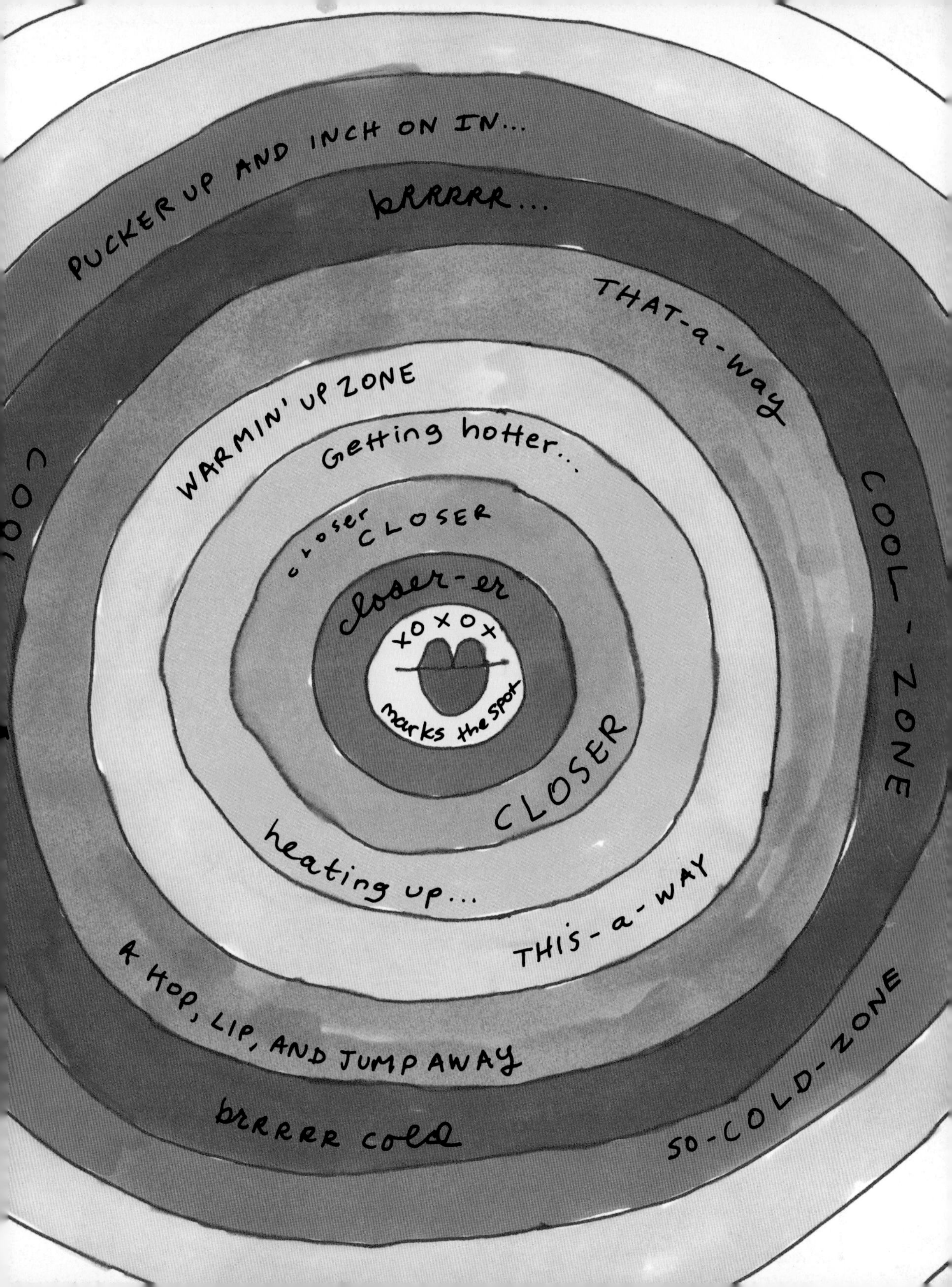
PUCKER UP AND INCH ON IN...
brrrrr...
THAT-a-way
COOL - ZONE
WARMIN' UP ZONE
Getting hotter...
closer CLOSER
closer-er
xoxox
marks the spot
CLOSER
heating up...
THIS-a-WAY
A HOP, LIP, AND JUMP AWAY
brrrrr cold
SO-COLD-ZONE

NOTE: This picture is not nearly as **cute** as Max, but maybe that's good, otherwise I might be too nervous to kiss a piece of paper! WOW! Imagine being too nervous to kiss a piece of paper! • **BOY** oh **BOY** I really have it bad for this **BOY.** I definitely think Max is **the most adorable** boy in school. • **P.S.** I forgot to mention Max is also very smart and funny. •**P.P.S.** Max is also **charismatic** — meaning he has this crooked little smile that can **melt** you as quickly as FROZEN Strawberry - Banana Yogurt on a hot summer day. Liz — my **VBF** (Very Best Friend) — says Max has "**Star Quality**." • P.P.P.S. I agree with Liz, except I think Max is even cuter than a lot of stars. • You know what's **weird**? (No, not that I'm kissing paper imagining it's Max. Just look at that picture of Max — how cute he is — and you won't blame me one bit.)

What is weird is **this**: Now that I've announced to Liz that I am **in love** with max, I see him **ALL OVER SCHOOL**. Everywhere I go, there is **max, max, max**— like there are **10 of him**. (Hmmm. Would it be **good** or **bad** to have **so many Maxs**? I'd have **10 times** more of a **chance** of **snagging** him as **my boyfriend**— but then I'd have to **other girls**.) you're bump-**time**," Rachel has told me. "A **sign** are **meant** to be to- (**NOTE**: Rachel is **16** a **teenager** for **four years running**, so I feel Rachel knows **extra things** about **LOVE**.) • I am thinking about what Rachel told me, when— **KNOCK KNOCK KNOCK**— ther is a knock at my **bedroom door.** • I open my doo

share him with **9** • "It's **fate** that ing into him **all the** (Liz's older sister) **you** and **he gether**." • and has beer

a **crack**, and see... **Rachel** "What a **wacky coincidence**," I say. "I was **just** thinking about **you**."

"There are no **coincidences**," says Rachel, pushing the door open. • That's when I see **Liz** behind her. • "**Everything** happens for a **reason**," says Rachel, now lying on my bed, as if she's been there

a **gazillion** er been (my bed) reason I says Liz, sister, bounc-settling into that **reason** us **pointers** friend." •

imes. **However**, she's **nev-** ere (my room) or there efore. • "And there's a rought Rachel by today," lopping down next to her ing a few times before a **particular spot**. "And s... Rachel's gonna give on **how to get a boy-** NOTE: The way I have Max, Liz has a **crush** on Karl.) • "What you GIRLS Love Strat-

a **crush** on a **boy named** need is a

egy," Rachel explains

A Love repeat. "Al- Strategy?" I e**xan**dra," says Rachel, **especially enunciating** the "**xan**" part of my name—making my name sound like oyalty. "Ale**xan**dra," says Rachel, Have you ever thought about why **some** girls lways get the boy and others **DON'T?** •

Rachel raises an **expertly tweezed, perfectly arched** **eyebrow,** then says **nothing**—just **lays there**, awaiting my answer. • I **really admire Rachel** (right down to her **perfectly painted purple toenails**) and want her to think I'm **grown up** and **smart**, so I **strain my brain** to come up with the **right answer.** • Could it be? ... Hmm. Sometimes I **worry** that you have to be **stick-figure thin**—like some girls I see in school—to get a boy. Then sometimes I think these girls are **SICK-FIGURE THIN**—like **YIKES** thin! **THEN** there are times that I look in the mirror and worry I have **ELEPHANT THIGHS! I've read** how a newborn elephant can weigh as much as half of a ton!

nd an adult can weigh 8 tons! Curiously, elephants are one
f the few animals other than humans that CRY. What makes
hem weep? my guess: They're bummed they can't find
eans they can fit into comfortably—or maybe they're
ust hungry for a jelly donut. • "Well," I say to Ra-
hel," sometimes I worry you gotta be **super thin**
o get a boy." • "Rachel is on a **new diet**,"
ays Liz. • "But **NOT to lose**
weight. I'm a vegetarian," says Rachel,
hen she pulls out the elastic hold-
ng her long black hair back
in a ponytail,
and shakes
her hair
oose.

"I no longer eat anything **with a head**," Rachel says. • "Really? What about fish?" I ask. • "Fish have heads," Rachel corrects me, whil snapping her hair elastic back an forth on a thumb • "Oh yeah. Right," I say. • Uh-oh. I'm now nervous I'm sounding stupid to Rachel. • "So, how about **lettuce**?" I ask her. • "What?" • "Lettuce comes in a **head**, right? So can you eat lettuce?" I smile widely to show I am kidding. "Or how about potatoes — they have eye Or **corn**, which comes in **ears**?" • "Ha, ha, ha," laughs Rachel. "You are very funny." • (**Phew.**) • "Well, anyway, I continue, "last month I started a new kind of diet." **MY NEW KIND OF DIET:** I clipped photos of beautiful, thin women from magazines and taped these clippings inside our **refrigerator** so I wouldn't want to eat when I looked inside. (**NOTE**: I don't know if **I've** lost any weight yet, but my **brother Howie**'s been getting a bit chubbier.) • "Oh, Ale**XAN**dra!" says Rachel. "Don4 be an **idiot**!" And she snaps her hair elastic at my arm. • "**ow**," I say. "what did I do?". • " You **KNOW** you don't ave to be **thin** o get a boy! " ays Ra- chel. "**Puh-lease!**" She sighs oudly. "You just nave to keep one thing in mind." • Liz and I lean in very close. • "Boys ARe **VERY** different from girls," says Rachel. • **Duh,** I am thinking, even I know that! • I first learned boys were different waaaay back in my youth — when I was **5**. I caught a peek at Howie **peeing while standing up**. It looke like so much fun, I thought I'd give it a try • **Unfortunately** my mom was walking past the bathroom when I did. • Or maybe it was **fortunately**. That's when she first told me how a boy — unlike a girl — has a **whatcha mathingie**. • My next lesson in how we girls are different came at age **9-ish**. I was just giving up my **imaginary friends**, when my mom told me about "A Girl's **Secret Friend** Who Visits Her Every Month" — her **PERIOD**. • I couldn't wait to tell my Very Real And **Best Friend** Liz. • But Liz already knew because she has a cat named Winona — and Winona has a favorite toy: Rachel's **TAMPO** which she loves to swat around the living room with her **paws**. • Winona also gave birth to kittens, so Liz **ALSO** knew a lot about other boy/girl stuff that I — as a **catless girl** — did not know. • It was Liz who first told me — when I was 10 $^{9}/_{12}$ths old — about "**sleeping with a guy**" — and this **truly** freaked me out. • "What if you're sleeping with a guy," I asked, "and you **wake up** in the middle of it?" • Thankfully Liz is a patient friend. She slowly explained what this meant — the **unbelievable** details coming from a **reliable** source: Rachel. • Thanks to Liz, I also got to see nearly **naked men** very up close on her 11th birthday. • No, they did not jump out from inside of a **cake**. • They were hidden inside a very large purple envelope — given to her by Rachel. Inside this pretty envelope was this amazing calendar of **The World's Sexiest Firemen,** with each month bearing a Fireman nearly baring it all! Liz generously split it with me, giving me the **Fall** and **Winter** months. (Note: I have a crush on **January Man.**)•"Rachel," I say, "Liz and I already know that a boy is built **differently** than a girl!" • "Yeah, puh-lease!'" says Liz. • "Wait a sec," says Rachel, "That's **not what I meant.** I meant boys think differently." **Boys THINK?**" says Liz.

tampona

Winona

Rachel snaps her elastic hair thingie at Liz's thigh, then looks directly at me. "A lot of boys just want one thing from us girls, so they wind up acting like real animals around us." How true. Some boys can totally be animals.

WOLF BOY

Todd Eberling is a wolf boy. When he's not playing gory computer games, he's prowling after girls at partie sniffing around them and drooling onto the floor. And he's sly like a wolf becaus girls never know how they wind up with his paws all over them.

Bobby Ferguson is a puppy boy. He follows girls around at parties — wearing his trademark extra big baggy pants. He waits for you to sit down on the sofa, then cuddles up next to you, often putting his head on your lap and asking you to stroke his hair.

"So," says Rachel, "Before you ever even kiss a boy, you always have to make sure of one thing." • "That you didn't eat garlic for lunch," says Liz. • Rachel snaps her hair elastic at Liz. "No," she says, "you have to **be sure he likes you for YOU** — not the kissing. A lot girls get wiggy around boys, and worry we should be thinner or prettier or that we're saying dumb things."

PUPPY BOY

NOTE: WOW, I FEEL LIKE RACHEL'S BEEN READING MY MIND—OR MY JOURNAL!

"And," says Rachel, don't think we going on, we go on—you know, **kissing** and so this is where **Strategy Assign-** "because we have **enough** let a lot mor when it come stuff. And your **Love** ment comes ir

•"Ugh," says Liz, an assignment?"• "you're giving u "From now on,"

says Rachel, "you must always remind yourself wha you have to **offer** a boy, instead of what you **Do** have. For instance, Ale**XAN**dra, you should make a list of all your **good** qualities, like how **smart** and **fun** you are." • "Wait," says Liz, "Isn't that MY list?" • "Ha, ha," I say. • "And Ale**XAN**dra," says Rachel, "I want you to think about these

good things every time you start to think something **bad!**" • "But, isn't that being conceited?"I
ask. • "So, she shouldn't **lose weight?**" Liz asks. •
Liz! Are you saying I'm **fat**!?" I say. • Snap, snap
goes Rachel's hair elastic at both Liz and me. • "Lis-
ten up, you two!" says Rachel. "You guys don't need
to stop eating **pizza** to get a boy." • "Good, I love
pizza almost as much as **boys,**" says Liz. • "Better
than most boys," I add, giggling. • Snap, snap again.
"Shut up," says Rachel. "I'm about to give you guys
four very important steps to follow to get a boy.
**STEP ONE : Be confident. STEP TWO : If you can't
BE confident, at least FAKE confidence. STEP
THREE : Keep on faking confidence. STEP
FOUR : Become confident.**'" • Suddenly, Rachel's
cell phone rings. "Hey honey, the pizza's
here!" says a male voice on the other
end. • "Wow! He just mentioned pizza!"
I say. "What a **coincidence**!" • "There
are **NO coincidences,**" says Rachel. "Come on,
Liz. That was Dad. We gotta go." •
After they leave, I get out my journal, but...

① I **always** order the **best thing** to eat on any menu

② I can draw an **armadillo** ➤

③ If you're at a movie and the actors on screen are mumbling so you can't hear what they've said, it's **good** to be sitting **next to** me, because I am one of the few people in the world who understands always **MovieMumbl** I'm **funny** I'm **smar**

④ Rachel says

⑤ Rachel says

⑥ **Heck, I am smart.** ⑦ And funny. ⑦ And nice. ⑨ I never give away the punch line to Someone's joke even if I know it

⑩ I have **big brown eyes.** ⑪ And **long eyelashes.** ⑫ I have **super strong thighs** from jumping rope. ⑬ **All in all, I make a pretty **excellent fun friend** to my friends. ⑭ And I'm an excellent fun friend to **dogs.** They can **never resist me.** ⑮ Heck, dogs are **never** wrong — **I AM IRRESISTABLE!**

...this time, instead of drawing a pic- ture of that **famous object** of my **affection** (max) I draw a **different** object of my affection: **ME**. And all around my self-por- trait, I write all the **cool things** about me that would make Max **very lucky** to have the opportunity to **kiss me**.

I look at **my picture** and all the **stuff** I've written around it, and sud- denly I have this **urge** to give my- self a **big kiss**. (Note: It's a very quiet **mwaaaahless** kiss.)

MICROCOSMIC CHAPTER

Why is it if boys aren't particularly known for loving **FLOWERS**, we girls dab and spritz ourselves with all sorts of flowery scents in hope of attracting boys? **HUH?** What's with that?

Lately I've been thinking if we girls are soooo determined to wear plant life to attract boys, maybe we should try some- thing with more Proven Boy Appeal, like **"Just Mowed Football Field."** Or better yet, how about *"Eau de Mashed Potatoes and Gravy."*?!

Wilson football

SUPERFLUOUS ZENITHS OF KNOWLEGE (and other icky stuff in life)

Did you ever notice the word **BROTHER** has the word **BOTHER** hidden inside of it? • Coincidence? **I thinketh not.** • My big brother Howie is **always bothering** me — in oh **sooo many ways!** • "How goes it, **melba?**" he is saying to me. • Melba is short for **Melba Toast** — a thing that is **flat.** Lately Howie has made it a habit to **compare me** — and specifically my **chest** — to all sorts of **flat things.** Or sometimes Howie just **cuts to the chase** and says, "**Yo, Flattie,** " outright. • "It's going, it's going," I tell him. • We are in the middle of a **game of Scrabble**. It's now my turn. I have a **couple of options,** and I'm not sure yet **which one** to take. • "Hey, melba, **check this out,** " say Howie. He then takes a **slice from the pizza** we are eat ing and puts the **entire thing in his mouth,** except for the tri angle tip which he **wiggles** around at me like it's some **snake tongue tip.** • **Very gross.** • My brother takes **pride** in how he can eat anything in the **grossest** way possible. I've read how **pythons** swallow their food **WHOLE** —like a whole egg, or a whole rabbit! A python is even famous for trying to swallow animals that are **larger than its own head—** which is **exactly** something **Howie would try to do!**

PYTHON EATING COACH

Way to go, Howie!! 8 pieces at once!!

I shake my head in disgust at Howie, then look down at my Scrabble pieces. I keep staring at the letter "**Z**" that I have, eager to come up with a good "Z" word. The **letter Z** has a **ten-point value**, which I think Z **totally deserves**. The letter Z totally **rules!** • I've always had a particular fondness for **words with "Z" in them** — and also words with other little words hidden inside. As embarassing as this is to confess, I often sit in my room and **read the dictionary**, searching for new, cool words. • Like the word **SUPERFLUOUS** — which has the word "super" inside it. Plus, it has **FOUR** syllables, which makes it super fun to say — or "**superfunous**"? Anyway, what it means is "not really needed" or "extra." • Another **NEW** and **LOVED** word: **ACUTE** — which has the word "cute" in it. It means "intense" or "pointed." • Then there's "**PHLEGMATIC**," which has the word "phlegm" in it — you know, that **gross green stuff** you cough up when you're sick — and looking at it makes you **even sicker!** It means "**slooooow**." • Well, I guess my brother thinks I'm being phlegmatic in

crabble, because he is now **screeching** like a
monkey. • "Hurry up and put down your word,"
says he, "or I'm gonna screech for as
long as it takes you." Then he screech-
creeeeeeeches! • Aaargh! Howie is sooo
annoying. (NOTE: I've read how chimpanzees have
98.4% of the same genes as a human—which is
kind of surprising, except in Howie's case.) I
quickly put down the word **"zenith."** • "That's
not a word," says Howie. • "Yes, it is. I just read
it in the dictionary yesterday. It means
the top of something, the peak." • "I can't
believe you read the dictionary. You're such
Brains Geek." • Howie hates school—
probably because he gets Cs and Ds
most of the time. A few months ago my
parents promised him a **bike** if
he'd get **better grades**. (Can you
believe he **weasled** that deal?)
And guess **what**? He **did** do
better—so he got a new
21-SPEEDER.

21-speeder
on a
zenith
of a
hill-
side
↑

That does not seem fair. I get **good grades** all the time. Meaning? I can't do anything to get a **freebie**! Part of me wants to start doing **really badly** so I can get a new bike, too! • "Hey, Flattie, you've got to put down a **different word**," says Howie. • "But that **IS** a word," I insist. • "Move it, Flattie," says Howie. • "Mom!" I yell out. "Mom! Tell Howie to stop calling me Flattie!" • "Howie!" my mom yells out, "stop calling your sister Flattie!". • "Melba..." he whispers. • "Mom!" I yell out, "he's **not stopping!**". • "Hey, I called you Melba not Flattie!" says Howie. • "Mom!" I yell. • "Howie!" my mother yells back. • "**Tsk, tsk,**" Howie whispers. "You've left me **no choice.** I'm gonna have to get you into **trouble**." • And I know he really means it. • **OKAY.** Let me tell you 2 more things about my brother Howie. →**2 MORE THINGS ABOUT MY BRO-THER HOWIE:** Although

Howie **stinks** at school, he **does excel** at ① basketball ② the art of torturing me. He's especially a **GENIUS** in this **#2 category**. In fact, it should really be listed as his **#1 category**. For example, look at what he is doing **RIGHT** now to me—or rather what he is doing to **HIMSELF**. Howie is biting **HIMSELF**—so now he's got big **TEETHMARKS** on his arm. Now he's running up to the kitchen to show my mom. "Look at what your daughter did!" he tells Mom. "**SHE BIT ME!** Really hard. It hurts!". "I did **NOT** bite you," I yell. "**DID** so," says Howie. "Did **NOT**. You bit yourself," I say. "Why would I bite myself? That's **stupid**," he says. "You're stupid," I say, then I hit him in the arm. (Can you blame me?!) Howie then hits me back in the stomach—leaving me **no choice** but to kick him in the leg. "Ow! Alex just kicked me!" Howie moans.

"That's enough," says Mom. "Alex, go to your room." "**Me?**"

"**Me?**" I repeat. "What about **Howie?** Howie started all this." • "I said go to your room!" Mom says. • Not **again**, I am thinking, as I march off to my room. Why does this **always** happen? Why do my parents always wind up believing Howie and **not me?** • So here I am ... Stuck in my room, while Howie runs **wild** and **free.** • I stomp over to my big box of beads and start making myself a **black bracelet** (to match my **mood**). But I cannot concentrate. I keep thinking about my life. • Hmmm. "**LIFE**" has the word "**IF**" squooshed inside it. Look. See? L...**IF**...e? • How **symbolic** to have this "**IF**" inside, because life is full of "**If only this**" and "**if only that**"! Like ... **If only** I did not have Howie as my brother. • **If only** I had a **cool sister** like Liz gets to have. • **If only** Liz were **my sister.** • **If only** Max, **adorable Max**, were **my brother.** (Wait. **No**. I take that back. That would be **gross**. I prefer to have Max as a **crush**.) • **If only**

I understood what happened between me and Howie. We used to be **waaay tight**. · I remember when I was 3 or 4, I cut off all the hair on my **favorite girl doll** and called it **Howie**—which was meant to be a big **compliment**. It was **weird**, too, how much this doll looked like him after the **haircut**. I used to carry my Howie doll with me **EVERYWHERE**, because I **LOVED** this doll and him **so much**. · But lately my Howie doll serves **another** purpose: I now use it to hold up the **loose window** in my bedroom on hot days like today. · **I look at my Howie doll—stuck in my window—its neck bent and twisted—and think about how bad things have gotten between Howie and me.** · **WHY** does Howie act so **mean** to me some-times? There are times I think he even **hates** me. And I **hate** being **hated**. Though sometimes I think I even hate him **right back**. And I **hate hating** someone. · I am thinking about this whole icky Howie situation

Mrs. Klein

substitute teacher

as of last Tuesday

...when I fall asleep, I'm somehow **STILL** thinking about it when I wake up. When the time comes to walk to the school bus, I do not want to walk with Howie. And I definitely **do not want to sit near him.** Thankfully I have Liz to sit next to. (And not just because her name has my favorite letter Z in it — but just **becauzzzze!!!**) My first class of the day is with this substitute teacher Mrs. Klein — we've had since last Tuesday. Today Mrs. Klein is teaching us how to "conjugate a verb." **FOR EXAMPLE:** the present tense: I strangle Howie. the past tense: I strangled Howie. the future tense: I will strangle

Howie. • the past perfect tense: I have strangled Howie. • (Yes, **how perfect** ~~is that!~~) • Vicki, the girl who I think is the prettiest in school, is sitting a desk away, whispering to her friend, Susi, and me a bit. "Doesn't Mrs. Klein look like the **Bride of Frankenstein**," Vicki whispers. Susi and Vicki giggle. I don't though I know **why** they're giggling. Mrs. Klein has this huge **gray streak** running through her **black hair**. But I think they're being mean. I smile at Mrs. Klein as she hands us back our essays—until I turn mine over and see to my surprise a large F. • **AN F!** I can't believe I got an F! I've never gotten an F before! • All over the paper Mrs. BOF Note : Short for Bride of Frankenstein) has

Mrs. Bride of Frankenstein as of right now

circled all my favorite words with red pen. At the
top she's written: "Next time don't have your parent
help you write your paper." • I am thinking: I
will strangle Mrs. B.O.F. I **have strangled** Mrs. Bo
mrs. B.O.F. **has been strangled**. • I stare at my pape
in shock—then quickly hide it in my notebook,
so Susi and Vicki cannot see it. • Finally, the bell
rings • I wait for everyone to leave the room, the
I head up to Mrs. B.O.F.'s desk. • "Excuse me, Mrs
Klein," I say, "I wrote this paper **all by myself.**

"Please, dear," she says, "the words in this story are n
the sort of words a 12-year-old girl would use
'**superfluous**' and '**phlegmatic**' and
'**acute**.'" • "But I **DO** use those words,"
I say. "I was reading the dictionary and
I really liked them, so now I use them." •
She looks at me like I am some **weird**
space alien. "Sweetie, I wasn't born
yesterday," she says. • I try to send bac

ALIEN THOUGHT WAVES

that say: really, this is true, really, this is true.
But mrs. Klein still refuses to believe me.
"If you rewrite the paper **YOURSELF**,"
she says, "without your parents' help, then
MAYBE I'll reconsider your grade." And
she leaves the room. • **WHOA**. • I cannot

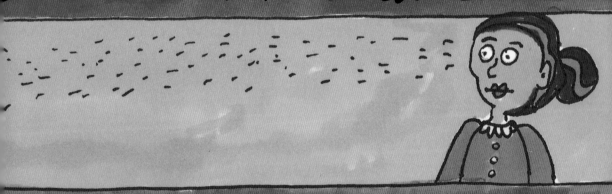

believe this. Luckily my next class is a
free study period. • I go and sit under
a tree. Again I find myself thinking
about the **unfairness** of my **L...IF...E**. •
Hmmm. Life also has a **BIG FAT F**
inside of it. • Next thing I know Howie
is standing over me. • "What's the
matter, doggiebreath?" Howie asks.
HOW DID HE FIND ME HERE?

I've read how some animals can **psychically** sense when a family member is **hurt**—even if this hurt member is miles away. For example, **dolphins** know when another dolphin is "**beached**"—meaning "on the beach out of water, sick and dying." The healthy dolphin will sense that its hurt family member is in pain, then seek it out and try to **save it**. • Maybe this is how and why Howie is here now. • Then again, I've also read about **vultures**. A vulture can sense when another animal is hurt, and seek it out —and try to **eat it**. • I look at my brother standing over me and **wonder**: Dolphin **or** Vulture? Vulture **or** Dolphin?. Howie sees <u>my</u>

Hmmm..
must
help!

...essay—which is lying out in the open on my lap.• "Wow, **you** got an **F**?" he says. • I study his face. I am looking for **clues**: Dolphin **or** Vulture? Vulture **or** Dol-phin?.• "An F? That **stinks**," Howie says—**seemingly very Dolphin-like**.•"Yeah," I say. "It's not fair. I worked hard on this paper!" • "Yeah, well," says Howie, "I work hard **all** the time—and get bad grades, too. Now you know how **I** feel." • "But **this** is **different**," I say. "I knew all those words! I really **did** do the work."•"Yeah, well, It's **not fair** because I work hard and **never** get A's," says Howie.• "Well, you know what's **unfair?**" I ask.

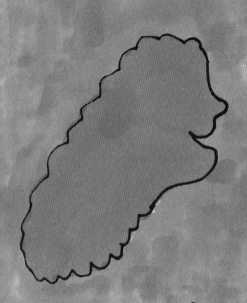

"Because you get **bad grades,** you get a **new bike!**"I say.

"Well, I've also gotten ground ed from basketball practice because of my bad grades- when I sometimes **work even harder** than you do! I've seen how sometimes you hardly work **AT ALL** and you **STILL** get A's!" says Howie.

"Well, it's **not fair** that Mom and Dad always believe you and your **stupid lies** about me doing **bad stuff** to you—when I don't ever do **anything bad** to you!"

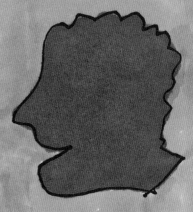

"Right! You're sooooo **perfect**!" says Howie. "And that's why Mom and Dad **love you more** — which is totally 100 million percent not fair!"

'They don't love me more', I say.

'No they don't. Especially not ately — when you keep getting me into **trouble!"**

"Yes they **do**!" Says Howie.

"**Good!**" says Howie. "My getting you into trouble makes things totally **fair**."

'What?'

"It helps to even things out so you don't seem **so perfect**."

So that's why Howie acts so mean and tries to get me into trouble. He's trying to get our parents to love me less, hoping they'll have a little extra love left over to give to him.
Howie's Just Jealous

...e thinks I have it so much better — which is **very funny** (ha, ha, ha) because my life is **icky** & a lot of the time. But Howie doesn't see this. Wow. Whoa. Hmm. Maybe this F isn't such a bad thing, if it's helped me see this new thing about Howie.

perhaps this F will help to reunite Howie and me. I hope.

So right then **I decide:** I will **remove** my Howie **doll** from my window sill when I get **home.**

"Ha, ha!" Howie then says. "I can't wait to tell Mom and Dad about **YOUR BIG FAT F!!"** Then he starts laughing this really evil laugh. • **Vulture!** That's it. Forget it. • The Howie doll **stays stuck** in the window until further notice.

MICROCOSMIC CHAPTER

You know who my hero is when it comes to LOVE?

The Tungara frog. I've read how if a female Tungara frog wants a boyfriend, she'll just boldly yell out →

Tung-ara-ara-ara!

But here's the catch to her mate-catching: All this Tung- ara- ara- ara talk can also attract

predators—

other animals who will try to kill her. But she doesn't care. The Tungara frog— romantic amphibian that she is—wisely knows that, heck, LOVE is worth the RISK.

Note:

I too feel that way in my heart but, somehow, for some reason, my mouth can't always seem to follow.

tale #3

TALK MUCH?

Here **I am,** sitting in **my bedroom** wondering: Wa there ever **a time** I was **happy, carefree,** singin **TRALALALA?** • It's **amazing** how much has changed in **16 days.** Yes, only a mere **384 hours ag** Liz and I **dared** each other at lunch to go up to a **crushes** and **(gasp!)** speak. Liz then **immediately,** **bravely** bolted over to Karl, sat **right down,** and started **talking.** • **Me,** I was a **slower go-er.** • I was scared. • I **tried** to remember Rachel' **Big Speech** on being more **confident.** I even tried t psyche myself up by reviewing **My Best** **Qualities List.** And it kinda worked— until I looked up, saw that Max was takin his **final bite of ice cream sandwich,** and knew it was "**now or never**" to make my move. • But **did** I move? • Naaah. •

I JUST SAT THERE AS FROZEN
AS THE SANDWICH MAX JUST FINISHE

Then he wiped his face with a napkin, and I somehow managed to get myself to stand. • He grabbed his books. • I got myself to walk (**slowly**) towards him. • He started heading for the **exit door**. • I switched plans and headed **his way**, so we'd both "coincidentally" leave **at the same time**. • Then there we were at the exit. • Our eyes met. • I said, "Hi." • Well, that's an **exaggeration**. I was **too nervous** to get out the **whole word** "Hi," so I only got out **half**. • "**H**," I said. • Max stared at me like I was weird. Maybe he thought my "**H**" was a **quiet belch**. • Next thing I knew I was standing there **alone**. • I quickly searched the cafeteria for **signs of Liz**, and saw she and Karl were still **talking, talking, talking**. • And they've been talking, talking **ever since**.

What's with

Why didn't Rachel's **pep talk pep me up?** It **pepped up** Liz so much she's never been **peppier.** I am so **jealous** of Liz's **bravery** when it comes to boys. Whenever I'm around boys, I can **NEVER** talk. (Note: I know I can talk around Howie, but he's more Monkey Boy than Human Boy.) Whenever I'm around a **real, human boy,** my brain goes **staticky—** like TV without the **cable hook-up** or like when you're trying to call up info about a Web site, and it takes **forever,** so you keep pressing the key, but the screen remains **frozen** with **NOTHING** on it. Well, THIS is my **brain around boys.** Liz, however, doesn't have **ANY** problem talking to boys—though she does now seem to have a **problem** talking with **ME!**

MY BRAIN

with GIRLS

I called her **2 DAYS AGO,** and she **STILL** has **NOT** called me back. • So here I am on a Sunday afternoon, sitting by the phone waiting for her to call. • You know what one of the **loudest sounds** in the world is? The sound of the phone **not ringing.** •

And you know what one of the biggest signs of **DORKDOM** is? No, it's **NOT** sitting by the phone waiting **boy** for a to call. It's sitting by the phone waiting for a **girl** to call! •

MY BRAIN with BOYS

I'm now afraid that since Liz hooked up with Karl, I'm no longer her **VBF**—but her **UTBVBF** (Used To Be Very Best Friend). • Suddenly I hear a **knock, knock, knock** at my door. • "Who is it?" I ask. • "Liz." • "Hmmm, Liz?" I say. "That name sounds familiar. I think I remember once

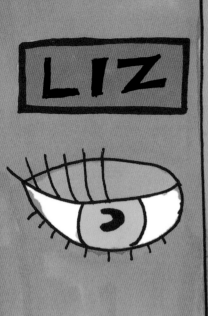

LIZ

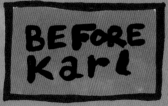

BEFORE Karl

knowing someone by **that name**." • "Shut up," says Liz, pushing open the door. She heads to my bed, grabs a magazine, starts flipping through. "What's new?" she asks. • I look over at her and think... **A WHOLE LOT IS NEW!** First there's Liz's new **bra (!)** that she's now wearing! Then there's Liz's **newly lip-sticked lips**. Liz's newly **mascara'd lashes**. Liz's **WHOLE NEW HEAD!** The left side of her hair is now noticeably **longer** than the right. • "You cut your hair," I say. • "Actually, Karl cut it," says Liz. • The sound of **Karl's name slice through me** like scissors through a certain someone's erfectly-Nice-As-It-Was-Before hair. • "Karl's very artistic," says Liz. "And talented at **painting skateboards**. He painted mine so you'd **barely recognize it**." • "I barely recognize **anything** about you right now," I **WANT** to say. • What I say instead is "**Uh huh.**" • "You know who I saw in a store yesterday?" asks Liz. • "No, **who?**" I say. • "**Max**," says Liz. • "**Max?**" **I repeat softly**. • "He was wearing these **dorky** orange pants," Liz says, giggling. "You should be **glad** you're not with him. He's **so five minutes ago**. make that **Sooo five seconds**." •

Liz

AFTER Karl

"Liz," I say, "I know you're trying to make me feel **better**, but you're **making me feel worse**, 'cause now you're saying: ① I have **stupid taste** in boys. And ② I can't even get a boy who is **sooo 5 seconds**." • "I'm sorry," says Liz. "That's not what I meant. I just want you to be **happy**." • "If you want me to be happy, you should've **called me back** when I called you!" • "**What?**". "I left a message with Rachel **two days ago**." • "I didn't get any message," says Liz. • "Yeah right," I say. "You were probably **too busy** to call me back, 'cause you had **important** things to do like **put on more lipstick** — and completely **change yourself** into this whole **differen** person — all to **please** some **dumb** boy."

"What? Alex, where is this coming from?" says Liz. "I changed all these things for me, not for Karl. I just was in the mood for some change—'cause change is fun, you know?" • I stare at Liz directly in her mascara'd eyes...but am at a loss for words. Gee, now not only can't I talk to boys, I can't even talk to LIZ! • "Look," says Liz, "my sister just gave me a box of her hand-me-down bras and makeup, so I started experimenting. Not because of Karl, but because it's fun—and good—to try new things. Look. I even brought you a bunch of her stuff. See?" • Liz unzips her knapsack, hands me a bulging pink plastic bag. • "Uh, thanks," I say. •

Does lip-stick mean LIPS are stuck? (puh-lease!)

"And I **swear** I didn't know you called," says Liz. • "Really?" I say. • "**Really**," says Liz. "Look I came by today because I want you to come to the movies **with Karl and me**." • "You're just inviting me **now**, 'cause I made you feel **guilty**," I say. • "No, you **big goofball**, that's **why I came over** I'm here, right?". • "Yeah.". • "So, can you come with us?".

US?! I thought Liz + Me = US

us? us? us?
us? us?
us? us?
us? us?
us? us?

us?
us? us?
us? US?
us? us?
us? us?
us? us?

Now Liz + Karl = US?!

"Shut up," says Liz. • "I didn't say any-thing," I say. • "You don't have to."

says Liz. And she grabs my hand and starts **dragging me out the door.** What is **REALLY** going on with Liz, **I wonder...?** Karl only lives nine blocks away, so we walk. His house has

us? us? us? us?
us? us? us?
us? us? us? us?
us? us? us? us?
us? us? us? us?
us?

one of those doorbells that plays a **whole stanza** of a song : **Dingdongdongdingdongdongdingdong-dong,** so long, Karl answers before it's even fin-ished. "Hey there!" he says. "Welcome to my **humble abode.**" (Then, finally, his **doorbell** stops ringing.) We walk into his living room. On the coffee table sits a **large glass tank** filled with a very **looong snake.** "Oooh gross," says Liz. "What's **Arnold** doing in **HERE?**". "He's watching TV with me," says Karl. "Hey, Liz!"

"Wanna pet him?" Karl asks. "Say hi!" • "No thanks!" says Liz, backing towards the sofa. • Karl snorts a laugh. • **I'll pet him**," I say. • "**Really?**" Karl asks, looking very surprised. • "Sure," I say. "Why not? He's not poisonous. **That's a corn snake, right?**" • "**Yeah!**" says Karl. • I lift the lid off the tank, reach inside, and **wrap the snake around my arm**. "Hi, Arnie!" I say. "You're cute." • "It's funny," Karl says, "how scared some people get around snakes when the average snake is no more **dangerous than a gerbil**." • "Yeah," I say, "it's a shame how **a few bad** poisonous **snakes** out there have **ruined** it for the rest of snakes." • Kurt and Liz both laugh. • "Has Arnie **molted** yet?" I ask. • "Yeah, a few times. I **saved it** in that box there." Karl points to a large metal box. Inside are a few coils of the snake's **shed skin.** • "Cool," I say. "I love the look of molted skin." • "**Me, too,**" says Karl. • "Just look at his coloring. Don't you just love all those orangey splotches?" • "Totally. And you know which snakes also **rule? Garters.**" "Yeah," I say. "That deep dark blue with stripes is **super cool.**" • And the next thing I know Karl and I are talking about which snakes we **love** — **and why.**

Boo!

• And the **next to next** thing I know Liz is **yelling at us**. • "Hey, we're gonna be **late** for the movies," says Liz. "You guys have been talking for over an **hour**!" • "**You're kidding!**" I say. • I look down at my watch. **WOW.** I can't believe it — I've been talking to a **BOY** for **over** an **hour**. • "**Come on, let's go,**" says Liz. "You two can talk **later.**" • Yeah I guess we **CAN** talk later. • **Maybe** I don't actually have a **problem** talking to boys! • It's funny how I've been **afraid** of **boys**, but I'm not **afraid of snakes**. I guess that's because I **understand** snakes, know what they are about. **Which means, I suppose, the things we are afraid of are the things** we do not **fully understand**, things that are **unfamiliar and new**. • I guess that's why I've been **so afraid** of all the **changes** Liz has been making — hanging out with Karl, wearing lipstick, cutting her hair all crooked — because these things are **NEW to me**. • But when you look at **change differently** — like see it as a sort of **molting** — then it's **not so scary**. • It's like this: I already know a snake molts its skin 'cause the snake is **growing** and **outgrowing** its **old self**, or rather its **young self** — and thereby becoming a **bigger** and **better** self. But..

IF YOU LIKED ORIGINAL LIZ YOU'LL LOVE NEW IMPROVED LIZ EVEN MORE!!
BIGGER! BETTER! OLDER! BOLDER!
NEW IMPROVED LIZ
NOW MORE FUN THAN EVER!
(with EXTRA Lizousity!!)
"NOBODY DOES LIZ LIKE LIZ"

...I guess if I didn't understand what molt-ing is, I'd be **afraid to see a snake molt right before my eyes**. But because I understand molting is about **growing**, and growth is **good**, well, then, molting seems **cool**. • And I look over at **Karl holding Liz's hand**, and suddenly I feel myself feeling **happy**. • "Come on, let's go already!" says Liz, dragging me out the door. • "Hey Liz," says Karl, "I like your friend, Alex. **She's fun.**" • "I know," says Liz. • "Hey, Karl," I say, "I like your friend, Arnie. **He's fun**. Oh...and Liz is pretty cool, too." • Liz sticks her tongue out at me. • "You know," says Karl, "There's this guy at school, a buddy of mine—he has a **really cool snake**—a black and brown **6-footer**." • "Let me guess. A **Ball Python**," I say. • "Right on. Exactly," says Karl. "Yeah, it belongs to this kid, Max Goldfarb" • Max—**my Max**—has a **snake.**

I give Liz a look and she gives me a look—and neither of us

MY SMILING LIPS..

I has to say a WORD, because, well, when you're VBFs...

... sometimes you just don't need to TALK. And I am HAPPY to be

HAPPY NOT TO TALK.

here in this moment- a moment of happily not talking.

MICROCOSMIC CHAPTER

Do you hear **that**? That **boom-de-de-boom-tra-la-la** music? • I hear it loud and clear. It's playing **inside my head**. And **now** because I can't stop **hearing it**. I can't stop singing it. • "**Boom-de-de-boom-tra-la-la**," I've been singing all morning—in the bathtub, picking out my underwear, tying my shoes. • I've read how the male humpback whale spends six months of each year **singing round-the-clock**. He just can't stop! • Yeesh! • I hope that's not gonna happen to me—not only for my sake, but for **EVERYONE** else's be- cause, well, to be honest, my voice is kinda **icky**. Fortu- nately for all the fishes

in the ocean, **the male humpback whale has a BEAUTIFUL voice**. And he even sings using **pretty rhythms and verses that rhyme**—just lik we use in **songs**! • Birds, too, compose songs with the same notes, rhythms, and harmonies of **modern music**! Actually, **all** of this is kind of **cool** when you **STOP** to think about it. (**Note**: Please stop now. I'll wait here.)— Are they **singing** because they're **happy?** Are they **singing** because they're **communicating?** Are they singing **because** they're so **happy** to be communicating? Just think: Animals as **different** as

BIRDS,
WHALES,
and
GIRLS
like
me!)—
we can
all find

ourselves waking up in the morning with this **UNCONTROLLABLE** urge just to **SING!**
...Boom-de-de-boom-tra-la-la-la!